Pa's Poopy Chair

Story and pictures by Niki Daly

CORGI PUPS

Series Reading consultant: Prue Goodwin,
Reading and Language Information Centre,
University of Reading

PA'S POOPY CHAIR
A CORGI PUPS BOOK: 0 552 546526

First publication in Great Britain

PRINTING HISTORY
Corgi Pups edition published 2000

1 3 5 7 9 10 8 6 4 2

Set in 18/25pt Bembo Schoolbook by
Phoenix Typesetting, Ilkley, West Yorkshire

Corgi Pups Books are published by Transworld Publishers,
61–63 Uxbridge Road, London W5 5SA,
a division of The Random House Group Ltd,
in Australia by Random House Australia (Pty) Ltd,
20 Alfred Street, Milsons Point, NSW 2061, Australia,
in New Zealand by Random House New Zealand Ltd,
18 Poland Road, Glenfield, Auckland 10, New Zealand
and in South Africa by Random House (Pty) Ltd,
Endulini, 5a Jubilee Road, Parktown 2193, South Africa.

Made and printed in Great Britain by
Cox and Wyman Ltd, Reading, Berks.

Contents

Chapter One

Pa Bombelly's studio chair
turned like a merry-go-round. It
was a very old chair. One day
when it made a "*peep*" sound, Pa
decided that it was time to buy a
new chair for the studio.

That night, a new do-it-yourself chair kit was advertised on the television.

"That's the chair for me!" said Pa excitedly.

Pa sent off his money and three days later a great box was delivered.

"It's broken!" said Bono.

"Send it back!" said Brenda.

"Don't be silly," said Pa. "It's a DIY chair. That means, to make it you must *do-it-yourself*."

Pa
started.
Wheels
went on the
round thing.

The round thing
was connected
to the pole
thing.

8

The pole thing got connected to the thingamajig, while the spongy seat got connected to the other end.

At last, the doodah got stuck on the thingamajig. And Pa stood back. "Try it out, Pa," suggested Bono.

Pa tried it out. He looked like a
rodeo cowboy on a hi-tech horse.

"That's a funny chair," said
Brenda.

"Maybe it will work," said Ma,
"if we wiggle the doodah."
Pa looked at the instructions.
"How's that?" said Ma.

"Can I try it out?" asked Brenda. She plonked herself onto the chair.

POOP!

"It made a rude sound!" laughed Brenda. Then Bono had a turn. "*Poop!*" went the chair.

POOP!

When Ma sat down it made a
louder "*poop*" sound.

"Come on, Pa!" they all
shrieked. "Take a seat!"

Pa looked embarrassed. He sat down very slowly on the spongy seat.

Slowly, a long and loud
"*Pooooooooooop*" squeezed out of
the chair.

Everybody shrieked with
laughter.

Pa looked fed up.

"*STUPID CHAIR!*" he yelled.

"But what a super box!"
said Ma.

Chapter Two

The telephone rang. Ma
answered it. "Irma Bombelly
here!" she said, sounding like a
woman on an advert. "Oh, hello,
Muriel," said Ma. "Yes, yes . . .
yes, yes, yes. Of course, we'd love
to have Nigel. Bye-bye, Muriel."

"Who's Nigel?" asked Bono.

"He's Muriel's little boy,"
said Ma.

"And who's Muriel?" asked
Brenda.

"Joe's wife," said Ma.

"And who's Joe?" asked Bono.

"My old friend," said Pa,
digging into a chest of drawers
for the photo album.

"Here," he said, pointing out two school boys. "That's me on the left and Joe on the right," explained Pa.

"Who's that?" asked Brenda.

"That's Granny Bombelly.

And this is Grandpa Bombelly,"
said Pa.

There was a photo of Ma
when she was a baby.

And one of Pa in a nappy.

There were photos of Brenda and Bono.

And there were many, many
more of cousins, uncles, aunts,
and others. Before they could
finish looking at their big family,
the doorbell rang and Pa closed
the album.

Ma answered the door. "Hello, Muriel," sang Ma.

"Irma!" chirped Muriel. "This is Nigel. Say hello, Nigel."

"*I want to go home!*" said Nigel.

When Muriel went off to have
her hair done, Brenda said,
"Come and look at Malcolm,
Nigel." So Nigel looked at
Malcolm. And Malcolm looked
at Nigel.

"I don't like cats," said Nigel.

"Let's watch the *Funny People Show*," said Bono, switching on the telly.

"*I want to go home,*" said Nigel.

"Do you like Lego?" asked Bono.

Brenda built
a dinosaur.

Bono built a
flying saucer.

Nigel built a wall.

"What shall we do now?"
asked Brenda.

"*I want to go home*," said Nigel.

When Nigel went to the
bathroom, Brenda whispered to
Ma, "Nigel's weird."

Bono said, "He doesn't smile,
he doesn't laugh and he doesn't
say anything."

"Except, '*I want to go home*',"
said Brenda.

"Well, he'll be going home
soon," said Ma.

When Nigel came out of the bathroom, Brenda made a funny hairstyle for him. Nigel didn't think it was funny.

Bono painted a face on his
tummy and made it speak. Nigel
didn't think *that* was funny either.

Then Bono and Brenda did their famous balancing act for Nigel.

Bono brought out his amazing
monster pop-up book.

Brenda stood on
her toes for Nigel
and wiggled
her nose for
Nigel.
But Nigel
said, *"I want
to go home!"*

At three o'clock Muriel turned up. "Hi, Irma!" said Muriel. "Thanks for looking after Nigel."

"Oh, it's been a pleasure," said Ma. "I do like your hair, Muriel."

Then Ma and Muriel started
chatting.

"*I want to go home!*" moaned
Nigel.

"In a minute, dear," said
Muriel.

"What a nice chair, Irma. Go
and get your cap, Nigel."

Nigel got his cap. *"I want to go home!"* he moaned, plonking himself on Pa's silly chair.

"*Poop!*" went the chair.

"Hey!" cried Nigel, jumping up.

As he landed back on the spongy seat it let out a louder "*poop*".

And still louder, "*POOP*".

"Time to go, Nigel," said Muriel.

Nigel looked at Bono and Brenda. A funny little smile crept onto his face. *"I DON'T WANT TO GO HOME!"*

Chapter Three

It was raining – plip, plop! The
raindrops fell against the wet
windowpane. Plip! Plop! Plip!

"I'm bored," sighed Bono.

"I'm *very* bored," sighed Brenda.

"Let's watch the *Great Brain Game Show*!" said Brenda.

Click! On went the telly.

A man with a big head was answering questions.

"He must be very clever," said Bono. "Look at his head."

"I bet he knows *everything*," said Brenda.

Another man with a small
head was asking lots of big
questions: "Who won the 1958
pig squealing competition?"

"*BORING!*" said Bono.

"Please switch off the television!" said Ma Bombelly, as she came into the TV room carrying a large cardboard box.

She put it down in front of
Brenda and Bono. "When I was
a girl and felt bored, my mother
always gave me a cardboard
box to play with," she said.

"When I was a boy, I never got bored," boasted Pa Bombelly. "I was always reading interesting things in my *A Thousand and One Amazing Facts* book."

"Such as?" asked Bono.

"Such as who won the 1958 pig squealing competition," said Pa.

"That's very interesting, Stanley," said Ma. "Who won?"

"Arthur Hamburger, of course," answered Pa.

"*BORING!*" cried Bono and Brenda.

Pa and Ma left Bono and Brenda with the box.

Brenda climbed into the box and closed the lid.

"Guess who I am?" asked Brenda in a spooky voice.

"You're Brenda in the box," said Bono.

"No, stupid! This is the voice of Madame X," said the voice. "And you will obey!"

"Go and fetch a cookie," ordered Madame X.

"I will obey," said Bono.

Bono ran off to get a cookie.
When he got back, the hand
of Madame X was waiting.
Bono handed over
the cookie.

"Crunch!
Crunch!"
went Madame X.

"I'm getting bored,"
complained Bono.

"I'm *already* bored," complained
Madame X, ". . . and
hot!"

The lid flew
open and out
climbed Brenda.

"Now it's my turn," said
Bono. He turned the box upside
down and bounced on it. "Guess
who I am," said Bono. *"Poop!
Poop!"*

"You're Nigel!" laughed
Brenda.

"And I don't want to go home!"
Bono joked.

"Let's watch the *Great Do-It-Yourself Show*!" said Brenda.
Click! On went the telly.

"Here's something for bored children to have fun with," said the DIY presenter.

Bono had an idea.

He ran to his room, fetched
his felt tips, and drew a window
on the cardboard box.

Bono asked Pa to cut out the window with a knife.

"What are you making?" asked Brenda.

"You'll see," said Bono.

When Pa had cut out the window, Bono drew on some buttons.

Next, he dug some things out of
his dressing-up box.

Then he placed the box over
his head.

Click! On went the telly.

"Who won the pig squealing
competition in 1958?" asked the
quiz master on the *Great Brain
Game Show*.

"I want a turn now," said
Brenda excitedly. Brenda was
the presenter on the *Great Do-It-
Yourself Show*. She explained how
to make a pig out of two toilet
rolls and a toothpick.

After that, they changed channels and Pa had a go. Pa read the news: "Mr Bombelly has decided to give his chair that '*poops*' to the first person who knocks on his door. Anyone needing a good laugh may contact him."

Bono and Brenda rolled on the floor with laughter. Ma came in to see what all the noise was about. Pa announced, "And now for the advertisements."

Pa took the box off his head
and placed it on Ma's.

Pa sat back and said, "I love
the woman on this advert."

"Hi!" said Ma. "Have you
tried Irma's muffins? Well, they're
scrumptious. They're ready! So
you had better eat them while
they're hot!"

Click! Off went the telly.

Ma's muffins were yummy and warm. They were all enjoying them when the telephone rang. Brenda ran to answer it.

"It's Nigel. He wants to come round!" whispered Brenda.

Bono looked at Pa and said, "I think Nigel must have seen Mr Bombelly's poopy chair on the news!"

Outside it was cold and
gloomy but not at all boring.
Nigel was on his way.

Ma's Muffins
Makes 12

Preheat oven to 180°C/350°F/Gas mark 4

Dry mixture

240g wholewheat flour
180g caster sugar
1 tsp baking powder
1 tsp bicarbonate of soda

Mix dry mixture together very well

Wet mixture

250ml milk
1 egg
50ml sunflower oil
140g raisins

Add wet ingredients
to dry ingredients
and stir

Spoon into a
greased
muffin tin

Bake for
20 minutes